# The WOOLY BIRD Meets
# Winnie-the-Pooh

## BY VINCE JEFFERDS

A GOLDEN BOOK • NEW YORK
Western Publishing Company, Inc., Racine, Wisconsin 53404

Christopher Robin and Winnie-the-Pooh
Were more like one than they were like two.
In sun or snow or stormy weather,
They loved to laugh and play together.

Anything Christopher wanted to do,
Was the very thing Pooh wanted too.

It seemed that whatever Chris would say,
Was what Pooh, in his very own way,
Was about to think of, anyway.

When Chris said, "Let's take a walk in the wood,"
Or "Time to take a little rest,"
It always made Pooh feel very good.
It was just what he was about to suggest.

And even on long rainy days
When Chris would study and read,
Pooh was always so amazed
How much he and Chris agreed.

$2 + 2 = 4$

If Christopher added on a pad,
His answers seemed just right
To the little bear, who couldn't add
(Or even read or write).

One day, when they went out to play,
A shadow fell across their way.
At first they thought it was a plane,
But the outline didn't look the same.

Pooh let out a frightened squawk,
"A hawk! A hawk! A hawk! A hawk!"

Christopher Robin began to run.
His vision was blinded by the sun.
When they reached the safety of the trees,
Pooh sat down to puff and wheeze.
"Christopher, can you tell me please,
Can anything at all be done?"

"An anti-hawk meeting
     is what we need."
"I think so too,"
     said Pooh. " Indeed,
That old hawk
     won't hurt us ever,
If we all stick together."

You could see that everyone was scared,
Except for Tigger, who declared,
"At this point I am announcing
I will give that hawk a trouncing!"

Just then a "whoosh" passed overhead!
Everyone froze still with dread.
Tigger, I'm ashamed to say,
Ran and hid in a pile of hay.

The bird landed before their eyes
And everyone felt like a fool.
It wasn't a hawk at all, besides,
It seemed to be made of wool.

They asked, "What kind of bird are you?
You must be a runaway from a zoo."
He answered, "Haven't you ever heard
Of a genuine striped Wooly Bird?"

"A Wooly Bird!
Why, that's absurd,
There's no such thing
As a Wooly Bird.
We think that it would be much better
If you were called 'The Flying Sweater.'"

"I'd like to come and live with you,
If there's some kind of work to do.

I'm not any kind of a shirker,
I'll work with a spade or a broom.
You'll find I'm a pretty good worker,
But don't ever wake me till noon."

So Kanga offered him work to do,
Baby-sitting with little Roo.

But Wooly didn't do it well,
He always had a story to tell,
And was forever leaving Roo
To find someone to tell it to.

And Wooly had the oddest way
Of making noises through his bill.
And there were things he'd do or say,
That came out even odder still.

He tried too hard to be a friend
With everybody in the wood,
And proceeded to offend
Because he was misunderstood.

He called on Owl
during the day,
But Owl told him
to go away.
(Owls have very
backward ways,
They hunt at night
and sleep most days.)

When Wooly gave another knock,
Owl finally undid the lock.
"There's no such thing as a knitted fowl.
This must be a dream," thought the sleepy Owl.

"Get out of here,
   you gaudy bird!
Stuffed mitten
   would be
   a better word."

Wooly offered Eeyore a worm.
But when poor Eeyore saw it squirm,
He gulped, and said he couldn't try it,
Because he was on a vegetable diet.

Monday was Tigger's bouncing day.
He asked Wooly along to play,
Then challenged him to a "bounce" contest.
"You'll soon find out that I'm the best,"
   bragged Tigger.

But Tigger didn't know at all
That Wooly could roll up in a ball,
So when he had to, just for fun,
He could bounce higher than anyone.

When Eeyore met Tigger
    later on,
He asked poor Tigger
    who had won
"The Wooly Bird did,
    but I'm still champ.
I didn't bounce well
    because of a cramp,"
    lied Tigger.

Poor Wooly bird, he never learned.
To Owl's roost he soon returned,
And proceeded to awaken Owl,
Who called him "a knitted nitwit fowl."

"I'll put you in a big plastic bag,
And sell you as a polishing rag
For very old broken-down cars.
Or better yet, I'll send you to Mars!
I have some cash that I can spare.
I'll gladly help to pay your fare."

While Wooly was at Owl's home,
Roo was left playing all alone.

With a "whoosh," a shadow crossed the sun.
"It's Wooly, back to have some fun,"
　　thought Roo.

But it wasn't Wooly, it *was* a hawk!
And before he knew it, Roo was caught.

Wooly heard Roo's frightened cry,
And came dive-bombing from the sky.
He hit the hawk so hard that Roo
Fell to the ground—and the hawk did too!

Everyone looked on,
  amazed.
The hawk and
  Wooly Bird
  lay dazed.
And little Roo,
  released and free,
Hopped quickly
  into a hollow tree.

Poor Wooly Bird, he tried to flee,
But found he couldn't because
The hawk had got his senses back
And caught him with his claws.

The hawk's sharp claw caught on a thread,
And Wooly Bird now found
The more he struggled to escape
The more that he unwound.

The farther he traveled
The more he unraveled.

You could clearly see where he had fled.
There was nothing left but a trail of thread.

In the wood, no word was spoken.
Roo and his friends were all heartbroken.

And birds flew in from far and near,
To pay their respects and give a cheer
For the odd little bird who, in the end,
Gave up his life to save a friend.

Kanga did not give up hope. Instead,
She quietly gathered all the thread.
And, because she was so clever,
She knit Wooly Bird back together.

What a surprise!
Before their eyes
The hero had returned.
And so our little Wooly friend
Got the welcome he had earned.